Roland Roberts

A Red Fox Book

Published by Random House Children's Books
20 Vauxhall Bridge Road, London SW1V 2SA

A division of Random House UK Ltd
London Melbourne Sydney Auckland
Johannesburg and agencies throughout the world

3 5 7 9 10 8 6 4

First published in Great Britain by
Hutchinson Children's Books 1993

Red Fox edition 1995

Printed in China

RANDOM HOUSE UK Limited Reg. No. 954009

ISBN 0 09 918691 8

For Stefan Bandalac

With thanks to the pupils and staff of the
Orchard County First School, East Molesey, Surrey

Rosie has started a new school.
She doesn't like it.
She doesn't like being a new girl.
She doesn't like sitting next to a BOY.
And she does not like Roland Roberts!

26a Tower Flats
Molesey
Surrey

Dear Grandad,
I hate my new school. It's very big and strange and I don't know anyone. Miss West the teacher is all right but she made me sit next to a BOY called Roland Roberts! At lunchtime she told him to look after me.

Roland Roberts said, "Girls are stupid." Girls are not stupid and I don't want him to look after me.

I hate Roland Roberts!

At break we all went outside and ran around playing games. Some of the children were so rough that I fell over and knocked my hand. I only cried a bit. Roland Roberts said, "It didn't hurt you, cry baby."

It did hurt and I'm not a cry baby.

I hate Roland Roberts.

When Mum came to meet me out of school, she started talking to Mrs Roberts. She asked her to come to tea one day soon so that Roland and I could play together.

Roland Roberts said, "Yuk!" I made a horrible face. I'm not playing with HIM.

I hate Roland Roberts.

I took Annabel to school today.
At playtime some of the boys ran
off with her and threw her
into the tree. Miss West was
very cross and got her down
with an umbrella.
Roland Roberts said, "It wasn't
us, Miss."
But I knew it was,
horrible Roland Roberts.

Ugh! Mrs Roberts and Roland came
round to tea and I had to take
him to my room to play. I got out
my toy cars and garage.
Roland Roberts said, "I didn't
think soppy girls liked cars, these
old ones are brill."
He doesn't know anything,
stupid Roland Roberts.

I was very excited this morning
because it had snowed in the night
and everywhere was white all over.
At school everyone was sliding and
throwing snowballs. One hit me
right on my ear.
Roland Roberts said, "Good shot!
Are you all right Ginge?"
I'm not going to be called Ginge, by
silly Roland Roberts.

Mum and I went to the park on Saturday, we took my sledge. Roland was there with his Mum and Dad and their dog, Bran. I had to share my sledge with Roland! Bran barked and chased us through the snow, it was fun.

Roland Roberts said, "I wish I had a sledge. Shall we make a snowman tomorrow?"

I really like Bran, but I'm not too sure about Roland Roberts.

We made the biggest, fattest
snowman you ever saw. It was
nearly dark when we finished.
I took Mr Roberts' hat and put it
on top. He called me a cheeky
rascal and pretended to be cross.
Roland Roberts said, "My dad
thinks you're the cat's whiskers."
I suppose,
he's not so bad, Roland Roberts.

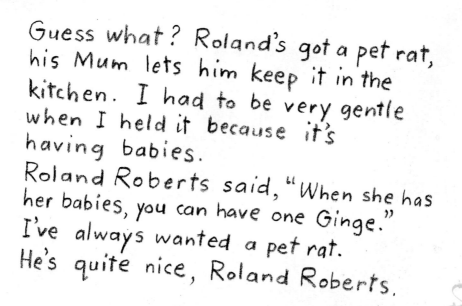

Guess what? Roland's got a pet rat, his Mum lets him keep it in the kitchen. I had to be very gentle when I held it because it's having babies.

Roland Roberts said, "When she has her babies, you can have one Ginge." I've always wanted a pet rat.

He's quite nice, Roland Roberts.

I showed Roland some photos of
me when I stayed on the farm.
He's never been on a farm and didn't
know that pigs could have thirteen
piglets. I told him that I was going
to be a farmer when I grow up.
Roland Roberts said, "So am I,
that's what I want to be."
He really likes animals,
I quite like Roland Roberts.

Now we are doing the Christmas play at school. Miss West said that if Roland doesn't behave himself he won't be Joseph.
Roland Roberts said, "I don't want to be Joseph unless Ginge is Mary."
Can I bring Roland to see you at the farm soon? He's my best friend.
I like Roland Roberts a <u>lot</u>!
        Love from
        Old Ginger Nut. X

Mr J Lee,
  Griggs Farm,
    Arklegarthdale,
    Yorkshire.

Some
bestselling Red Fox
picture books